MY FIRST
BOOK OF
BEDTIME
STORIES

This edition © Ward Lock Limited
1989

First published in the U.S. in
1989 by Ideals Publishing Corporation,
Nashville, Tennessee.

ISBN 0-8249-8382-3

All rights reserved. No part of this
publication may be reproduced, stored
in a retrieval system, or transmitted, in
any form or by any means electronic,
mechanical, photocopying, recording,
or otherwise, without the prior
permission of the Copyright owners.

Printed and bound in Czechoslovakia

MY FIRST
BOOK OF
BEDTIME
STORIES

Illustrated by

Margaret Tarrant and others

IDEALS CHILDREN'S BOOKS
Nashville, Tennessee

CONTENTS

MRS. BUN'S BIG WORRY

You know, don't you, that rabbits are timid
creatures. You know that they are very easily
frightened.

Well, Mrs. Bun is the most timid rabbit of
them all. She is *always* fretting and worrying
about something. She frets and worries so
much, she frightens herself!

Mr. Bun is the opposite. He stays calm, no
matter what. Each night Mrs. Bun stands in
her nightgown and worries out loud, "What if
burglars break in while we're asleep? What if
the house catches on fire? What if it rains and
the roof leaks?" But Mr. Bun just kisses her
on her soft pink nose and says, "Sleep well."

One night, she woke him up at five o' clock
in the morning. "Oh, Mr. Bun! I've had such
a terrible dream! I must tell you!"

Mr. Bun opened one eye and lifted one ear off the pillow. "Tell me your dream then, dear," he said patiently.

"I dreamed, I dreamed – oh me! It was dreadful! I dreamed the children had to do my shopping for me!"

"That doesn't sound dreadful," said Mr. Bun. "That sounds like a great idea." But he went on listening with one sleepy ear.

"I gave them some money and I asked them to buy me an onion and some carrots, a spoon and some nuts, a cabbage and six fresh eggs . . ."

Now for those of you who don't know, Mr. and Mrs. Bun have two children. It's easy to tell them apart: Currant has a little fluffy brown tail, and Cream has a little fluffy white one. Everyone knows what good, helpful little rabbits they are; and Mrs. Bun often asks them to help her around the house, dusting and polishing.

In her dream Mrs. Bun gave them a basket to carry the groceries and told them, "You must be careful. Walk, don't run. And don't play so that you drop the basket and spill the groceries and break the eggs."

"We would *never* do that," said Currant.

"Never *ever* do that," promised his sister Cream.

Off they went, as good as gold. They found the shop and bought the groceries – an onion and some carrots, a spoon and some nuts, a cabbage and six fresh eggs. And they set off for home again, carrying the heavy basket between them.

Currant and Cream didn't play on the way home. No, no.

They walked – they didn't run. Certainly they didn't.

In fact they were as sensible as two small rabbits can be.

But suddenly . . .

A great big black-and-white puppy dog came into sight, bouncing and bounding and barking. Of course Currant and Cream were terrified!

Would the puppy see them?

Would he chase them?

Would he bite them?

Quick as a flash, the two young rabbits hid behind a tree. How their delicate whiskers trembled as the noise came closer and closer to where they were hiding!

Fortunately, the puppy went bouncing and bounding and barking by.

Currant popped out from behind the tree and cried, "Come on, Cream! Let's get out of here before he spots us!" And he grabbed the basket and took a great stride toward home, all the time looking over his shoulder, watching out for the puppy.

So of course he didn't see the knotty tree root sticking up out of the ground.

Down he tumbled and down went the basket, too. Out spilled the onion, the cabbage, and the spoon. Out spilled the carrots and the nuts. But worst of all, out spilled the eggs:

Cr-plack! Cr-plack! Cr-plack!

All six of them broke into one big yellow squelch.

"Oh dear! Oh dear!" cried silly Mrs. Bun tugging on her husband's ears in terror. "If I send Cream and Currant shopping, my dream is bound to come true!"

"Nonsense," said Mr. Bun, refolding his ears on his pillow. "Send Cream and Currant shopping as often as you like."

"But the eggs will all get broken!"

Mr. Bun sighed. "So send them to buy onions and cabbages, carrots and spoons and nuts. *Only leave out the eggs*. Then if the basket gets dropped, nothing will break at all. Now wake me up when it's morning. Night-night."

WHEELIE WINNIE

"What's this? What's this?" cried Scratch Squirrel. She was perched up at the top of the tall pine tree in the middle of the woods, collecting nuts for the winter. But the tree began to shake under her.

The high branches shook so much that Scratch dropped one of her nuts.

As the little squirrel peered down through the leaves she saw a man was swinging a long, heavy axe. With each blow he cut a big notch out of the tree's trunk.

"Hey! You can't do that!" cried Scratch. "Don't you know that this is the Extra Special Tree?"

"That's why the toymaker asked us to cut it down," replied the woodcutter. "He wants to make an extra special toy."

Several men tied ropes around the tree and heaved until the great forest pine gave a groan and fell to the ground.

They cut it into logs and carted them away to the toymaker's yard. There the toymaker picked up one piece of wood after another and looked them over carefully until he found one that was just right.

Then he sawed it and planed it, he shaped and carved and turned it, he whittled and sanded it, he polished and painted it. He took some wool and some horsehair and some leather, too, and he made a mane and a tail and a bridle. Can you guess what kind of toy he was making?

Of course! A horse!

Finally he nailed on four wheels and a handle for pushing and stood the horse in the window of his shop. On a sign he wrote

AN EXTRA SPECIAL HORSE
FOR AN EXTRA SPECIAL PERSON

Ronnie was that extra special person.

His mother and father bought the extra special toy for their extra special boy, and on the morning of his birthday Ronnie found the wooden horse standing by his chair at the breakfast table.

Oh, there never was such a birthday present! Ronnie had always wanted a horse of his own.

"Will she let me ride her? Will she gallop? Will she trot? Will she canter? Will she rear up and snort and snicker? Will she whinny?"

"That sounds like a name – Wheelie Winnie!" said his sister Jane, laughing. "You should call her Wheelie Winnie – because she has four wheels and horses whinny when they're happy!"

So that's what the horse was called. And Ronnie says he heard her softly whinnying that very night as if to say, "I'm very happy here in my new home."

Baby wanted to ride Winnie.

Of course, Ronnie had to say yes because children must always be ready to share their toys. But Baby's legs were too short to reach the ground when he sat astride, and he rolled off and bumped his head and cried. So he was not allowed to ride Winnie again.

Jane wanted to ride Winnie, too. But her legs were too long; they got in the way.

So only Ronnie could ride Wheelie Winnie, because he was just the right size. He was secretly pleased about that. So was Wheelie Winnie.

"We shall go on lots of adventures together and fight battles and explore dangerous places and race the wind," whispered Ronnie. He built Winnie a stable out of boxes beside his bed. As he dozed off to sleep, one hand resting on Winnie's woolen mane, he thought he felt the little horse nod and he heard her whinny with joy.

ELFRED THE
DRAGON RIDER

It seemed like an ordinary day.

John only meant to go out for a ride in his toy car, then come home again for lunch. He only stopped beside the Old Oak Tree because it was such a hot day and the shade looked so cool. As he sat there, his back against the trunk, he watched the dragonflies dart to and fro through the tall grass.

When he saw him, he had to blink once and look again because he was such a very odd sight. But there he was! Astride one of the dragonflies sat a little elf, dressed in a green tunic and a pointy red hat. Everything about the elf was pointy – his sharp little nose, his sharp little ears, the toes of his boots. And he was pointing at John as if to say, "Giddyup, dragonfly! He's the one!"

The dragonfly landed right on John's knee, and off hopped the elf. "I'm Elfred the Dragon Rider. You look like a giant, so I'd better fight you and cut off your head!"

"I'm not a giant," said John quickly. "I'm only a little boy. And I don't want to fight you. I'd rather be friends."

"Whew. That's lucky!" exclaimed Elfred. "If we're going to be friends, you should come and visit my home. That's what friends do. Oh, but you'd better eat this first."

Elfred took a tiny red apple out of his pocket and gave it to John. At the first tiny bite John started to get smaller and smaller, until he was no bigger than Elfred himself. Then off they flew.

The elf's home was a tree house at the top of the Old Oak. Elfred and John had to climb up a rope ladder to reach it, but it was worth the effort because there were bowls of strawberries waiting for them.

"Delicious!" said John. "But I must be going soon, or people will start to worry. How do I get big again?"

"Oh dear," said Elfred. "I've never done that magic before. I don't know."

"Well, who does?" cried John. "I don't want to be this small forever!"

"Don't worry," said Elfred. "Let's visit Wizard Woops. He'll know the magic spell."

So they went to visit the old wizard, and he mixed a magic potion for them in a big cooking pot over the fire.

The magic potion tasted very nice – like bananas and honey – but it didn't make John big again.

"Oh dear," sighed Wizard Woops. "This *should* be as easy as flying. All you need is a special magic word from my Great Dictionary of Magic. But I'm afraid More-Gone the Pirate stole it. You will just have to go and find More-Gone and get the book back."

He took them outdoors, where the leaves looked as big as row boats to people as tiny as Elfred and John. The wizard sprinkled magic over two of the leaves, and at once they floated off the ground. "Climb in and hold tight!" said the wizard. "These chariots will take you wherever you want to go."

"Take us to More-Gone the Pirate!" cried Elfred, and their leaf-chariots carried them over hills and rivers, deserts and seas to where hot, sandy islands poked up out of a blue ocean. There, in the distance, lay the pirate galleon, and tied to the mast was a tiny yellow-haired prisoner – a beautiful girl elf.

Down they swooped between the sails and ropes to the deck of the galleon. The ship was deserted. All the pirates had gone ashore to bury their treasure. So John freed the pirate's prisoner (whose name was Elfleda) and she clambered aboard his leaf-chariot.

"To the beach!" cried John.

"Thank you for rescuing me!" whispered Elfleda in John's ear.

"You're welcome," said John. "Do you know where More-Gone has hidden the Great Dictionary he stole from Wizard Woops?"

"Oh, yes. It's in that treasure chest — the one they are burying in the sand now."

So Elfred and Elfleda and John simply waited until the pirates had gone, then dug up the treasure chest and found the book.

"Here's the magic word," said Elfred. "To get back to where you started, all you have to say is . . . but wait, you will come and visit us again, won't you?"

"Of course!" cried John.

"Heckleflecklepop," said Elfred.

"Excuse me?"

"That's the word. You just say —"

"Heckleflecklepop!" said John, and found himself sitting in the shade of the Old Oak, just as big (or as little) a boy as ever.

CURRANT, CREAM, AND EGGS

"I would really enjoy an egg for my dinner!" said Mr. Bun, forgetting how Mrs. Bun loved to worry.

"Oh dear, oh dear. But if I send Currant and Cream to the store, they might drop the eggs on the way home. Oh, the waste of money! Oh, the waste of eggs! Oh dear!"

"Never mind," said Mr. Bun sadly. "It really doesn't matter."

Currant, overhearing this, whispered to his sister, "Why don't we get Dad an egg for his dinner. Mrs. Hen might give us just one, if we ask nicely. Then Ma will see how we *can* carry eggs home safely without breaking them."

They had only got as far as the crossroads when they met Mrs. Hen. "Please would you give us one of your eggs as a surprise for our Dad?" asked Cream sweetly.

"I'll give you six eggs if you will help me look for my chicks!" wailed Mrs. Hen jumping from one foot to the other. "I just turned my back for a moment, and they wandered off! Now they are lost, lost, lost, and it will be dark soon. Then what will become of my poor little ones?"

"Don't worry," said Currant. "I'll take this road, Cream will take that road, and you can take the third. Between us we'll search until we find your lost chicks, Mrs. Hen."

They searched and they called; they called and they searched. But whenever Currant or Cream saw a fluffy speck of yellow in the grass, it popped out of sight before they could reach the spot.

"I think those naughty chicks are playing a game and hiding from us," said Cream to Currant.

"Well, I'll soon put a stop to that!" said her brother.

Currant coughed and said in a loud, loud voice, "Come along, Mrs. Hen. Come along, Cream! It's getting very dark and it is foolish to be outdoors after dark. There are *foxes* and *weasels* and *owls* and all sorts of *dangerous animals* out hunting for something small and delicious to eat. Hurry! Let's go home!"

And taking Mrs. Hen, one by each wing, they rushed her home, despite her loud, squawking protests.

As they went, though, Currant and Cream made very sure to flash their fluffy tails in the twilight so that the naughty little chicks could keep sight of them and follow on behind without getting lost.

In their hiding place in the tall grass, Pick and Peck looked at each other and shivered. "*Foxes!*" they exclaimed.

"*And weasels!*"

"*And owls!*"

"*And other dangerous animals!*"

When Currant and Cream got back to Mrs. Hen's house, they pretended to lock and bolt the door. "Home is the only safe place to be after dark!" said Cream in as loud a voice as she could manage.

No sooner had the two little rabbits sat down, then there came a desperate *knock, knock, knock*. In tumbled Pick and Peck. "Oh, Ma! Oh, Ma! We won't ever wander off again! Why, we might have been eaten up by *foxes* or *weasels* or *owls* or some other *dangerous animal*!"

Of course, Mrs. Hen tried to be cross, but she was just so happy to see her children again. Then she filled the basket with fresh eggs; it was so heavy that Currant and Cream had to carry it between them. "Hurry home now. It really *is* dangerous to be out after dark," said Mrs. Hen. "And be careful not to drop the basket." She did not understand why the two little rabbits giggled.

The little family of chickens stood on the steps to wave goodbye. But of course Currant and Cream could not wave back because they were carrying the eggs so very carefully.

"I wish I had a fluffy white tail like Cream," said Peck.

"I wish I had a fluffy brown tail like Currant," said Pick.

"When you are grownup, sensible chickens, you will both have great big tails like bright feathery fans," said their mother, ". . . but only if you keep away from *foxes* and *weasels* and *owls* and don't run off and hide in the tall grass."

I think the chicks learned their lesson.

But what do you think happened to that full basket of eggs? Did it reach home safely? Did Mr. Bun have his surprise dinner? Did Mrs. Bun stop worrying about sending Currant and Cream to the store to buy eggs? I do hope so.

THE GREAT RACE

One day Ronnie was out riding his wonderful wooden horse, Wheelie Winnie, when they met Scott, the boy who lived next door. Scott was riding a new, shiny red scooter, and how fast he went.

"*Vroom!*" roared Scott, and he charged right at Ronnie and banged into him. It might have frightened Winnie had she not been so very brave.

"Silly old donkey!" shrieked Scott. "You call that a horse? Why it's just a silly old wooden donkey!"

(Scott was not a very likeable boy.)

"She's not! She's the best horse in the whole world!" said Ronnie angrily.

"Prove it then," said Scott. "Let's have a race. Race you! Race you! Race you to the bottom of the hill! Or are you too scared?"

Now Ronnie could sort of feel through his knees that Wheelie Winnie did not like the idea. But Scott only sneered and jeered, "Scaredy-cat! Won't race! Doesn't dare!"

Well, that made Ronnie so mad he decided to do it.

They started the race right at the top of the hill. Ronnie tucked up his knees and Winnie rolled faster and faster on her round wooden wheels. But she was not as fast as Scott's scooter! He went hurtling down the hill too fast to stop!

At the bottom of the hill, Scott's scooter skidded one way, and he slid another. A moment later Wheelie Winnie crashed into the scooter and Ronnie went down too.

What a disaster! When Ronnie picked up his beloved horse, one wheel was off and all the paint was scraped on one side.

"Looks bad," said Mr. Baker, who had been watching the race.

Scott ran home crying, leaving his scooter in the road. Ronnie didn't cry. He was too worried about Wheelie Winnie.

But Mr. Baker, who had seen the accident, found a nail and took a big stone and banged the wheel back on. Then Ronnie wheeled his horse home very gently and took her to the shed. He found a can of paint and painted Winnie's stripes just as they had been before. He didn't tell anybody about the race or the accident until Wheelie Winnie was looking as good as new.

His mother told him he must *never* race down the hill; then she looked at the little wooden horse. "I'm glad that Winnie didn't hurt herself," she said " like that red scooter I saw all scraped and bent, lying in the road."

"I'm sorry, Winnie," whispered Ronnie in his horse's ear. And it seemed as if Winnie shook her head and said, "That's all right – just don't do it again!"

DRAGON WEDDING

One day John met his friend Elfred under the Old Oak. The little elf was bursting to tell him an exciting piece of news.

"The Sea Dragons are getting married! I heard it from the Mermaids – they're the first to know anything that happens in Fairyland. Everybody is invited! Would you like to come?"

"Absolutely!" cried John. So he ate one of the elf's magic red apples to make him as small as an elf himself. "Who will I meet at the wedding?" he asked.

"Oh, everyone who's anyone: the Seagulls, the Fairies, the Seahorse, the Penguins – the Mermaids of course – and every dragon you have ever seen, naturally."

"I've never seen any dragons before," said John. "Will Elfleda be there?"

"Never seen any dragons?" cried Elfred. "What have you been doing all these years?"

"Are they very terrifying?" asked John as they rode through the air in their leaf-chariots toward the forests of Fairyland.

"Dragons? Not terrifying at all if you like green and don't mind them having two heads each."

"But what can I give them as a wedding present?"

"Oh, no need for that. Things are different in Fairyland. At weddings there, all the guests get presents instead — one wish each. The King and Queen see to that."

John would have asked more questions, but the sound of music grew too loud below them. They had arrived at the dragon wedding.

And what a wedding! It was sunset before the happy couple spread their four wings, nodded their four heads to thank everybody and flew away on their honeymoon.

Only after they had gone did the King and Queen of the Fairies arrive with a train of a thousand fairies. The King and Queen had shining butterfly wings of purple and white, and they wore golden crowns on their heads.

"They come later so the guests aren't distracted from watching the bride and groom," whispered Elfred. John could understand that – although he thought Elfleda was prettier than anyone there.

Soon the King summoned John to his throne. "We have heard much about you," he said. "How you rescued Elfleda from the Pirates and returned the Great Dictionary to Wizard Woops. Kneel down and I will dub you a Knight of the Order of Elves!"

So John knelt down as a little boy and rose as a Knight-Elf. In his excitement he almost forgot the magic word – *Heckleflecklepop* – that would take him out of Fairyland and back home again.

MR. BUN'S PIPE

"Oh dear, oh dear. I do worry about Mr. Bun smoking that old pipe of his. I'm sure it isn't good for him," thought Mrs. Bun one day. (You know how she loves to worry.) So when Mr. Bun put down his pipe, she hid it out of sight under the table.

Soon after, the family sat down to dinner, and Mrs. Bun bustled about in the kitchen, mumbling and muttering, "Oh I do hope the food hasn't burned. I do hope it's hot enough. I do hope I didn't use salt instead of sugar."

Then little Currant wrinkled his nose and started to sniff. "I smell a funny smell," he whispered to his sister.

Cream sniffed. "I smell it too," she said.

The two little rabbits peeped under the table, and what do you think they saw?

A curl of smoke and a lick of flame. "I don't like to worry you, Mother," said Cream gently, "but the carpet seems to be on fire."

"Oh my paws! Oh my ears! Oh my whiskers!" cried Mrs. Bun, turning as white as her tail. "It's all my fault! I hid the pipe! I've set fire to the house! I've burned down the very roof over our heads! We'll lose everything! We'll all die! And it's my fault! Oh, what a foolish rabbit I've been!"

While Mrs. Bun hopped about the room in confusion, Currant got a pitcher of water from the kitchen and put out the fire. "Well done, son," said Mr. Bun softly.

"Nothing to worry about," said Currant.

When they had finally persuaded Mrs. Bun to sit down and have a cup of tea, she promised she would never again hide Mr. Bun's pipe without asking him. "In fact," she said, "I'll never worry or fret ever again. It's far too dangerous!"

WINNIE TO THE RESCUE

Ronnie was glad when the rain stopped. For days and days it had been too wet to play outdoors, and he wanted very much to take Wheelie Winnie for a gallop in the park. Jane came too.

The ground was still very wet. The grass was muddy, and the path was spread with big round puddles. "Look over there!" exclaimed Jane. "That puddle is almost as big as a pond. And what's that in the middle of it?"

Crouched on a large rock in the middle of the puddle was a small black kitten. What a sad sort of a sound she was making, too!

Mew! Mew! Mew!

You see, the puddle had grown big around her, and she couldn't get to the edge. You know how kittens hate water! "Winnie will rescue her!" cried Ronnie.

He pushed Wheelie Winnie as far into the puddle as his arm would reach. The frightened kitten jumped upon Winnie's back, and Ronnie was able to pull her to the edge.

But oh! That little cat's claws dug sharply into Winnie's wooden back. And that water was so cold creeping around Winnie's wheels. There was a chance that the nails holding the wheels in place might go rusty, and then how would Winnie trot about?

"You are very brave!" said Ronnie hugging her painted neck. He saw her wet wheels and he rubbed off every last drop of water with a soft cloth, so that Winnie was as shiny as new.

"See how nice you look after your brave rescue!" said Ronnie, and he showed the little wooden horse her own reflection in a mirror.

And she had to admit, she did look somehow different.